EAT YOUR PEOPLE!

Windsor and Maidenhead

To my little monsters. **L.K.**

ORCHARD BOOKS

First published in Great Britain in 2016
by The Watts Publishing Group
This edition first published in 2017

1 3 5 7 9 10 8 6 4 2

Text © Lou Kuenzler, 2016
Illustrations © David Wojtowycz, 2016

The moral rights of the author and illustrator have been asserted.

A CIP catalogue record for this book is available from the British Library.

ISBN 978 1 40833 034 0

Printed and bound in China

MIX
Paper from
responsible sources
FSC
www.fsc.org   FSC® C104740

Orchard Books
An imprint of Hachette Children's Group
Part of The Watts Publishing Group Limited
Carmelite House, 50 Victoria Embankment, London EC4Y 0DZ

An Hachette UK Company
www.hachette.co.uk

www.hachettechildrens.co.uk

Lest we forget the plight of people everywhere. **D.W.**

EAT YOUR PEOPLE!

LOU KUENZLER

DAVID WOJTOWYCZ

ORCHARD

"Eat up, Monty!"
growled Mummy Monste[r]
"Otherwise there won't
be any pudding!"

"But I *hate*
eating people,"
moaned Monty.

"They're so **chewy** . . .

and **crunchy** . . .

and

full

of

bones!"

"Stop fussing!" said Daddy Monster. "You've only got a tiddly child-sized portion! One big MONSTER mouthful and they'll all be gone."

"But I **HATE** eating people!" groaned Monty. "They're so wriggly and jiggly. They keep waving at me.

YUCK!"

"I'll eat yours!" cried Monty's big sister, Monica. "People are my FAVOURITE! I've already finished all mine! Look!"

"Put that back, Monica!" said Mum. "Monty must eat up all by himself!"

"I'll eat ALL my vegetables!" said Monty. "But I WON'T

EAT MY PEOPLE!"

Mum stared hard at Monty. "No pudding
until that plate is *COMPLETELY* empty," she said.

Monty prodded his people with his fork.

"Don't play with your food," said Dad.

"I'm counting to **three,**" growled Mummy Monster.

"**One**

two..."

"All right! I'm ready!"
Monty gulped.

He popped a person
into his mouth and . . .

"**. . . YUCK!**" spat it back out again.

"They're so SOUR!"

Mum did not
look pleased.

Dad did not
look pleased.

Monica laughed so hard,
her drink came out of her nose.

"Can I just eat the heads?" begged Monty. "Or the feet?"

"No!" said Mum. "But if you eat everything up –
right now! – I'll give you an extra big

MONSTER-SIZE

helping of pudding.

It's your **FAVOURITE**."

"My *VERY* favourite?"
asked Monty.

"Yes," promised Mum.

"In that case," said Monty, "here goes!"

He scooped up
ALL his people in one

BIG,

chewy,

crunchy,

wriggly,

jiggly,

sour . . .

MOUTHFUL!

"Well done!" said Mum.

"YUCK!" Monty wiped his mouth.

"ALL GONE!" he said.

Then he held out his plate for a

giant monster-size

helping of his FAVOURITE pudding . . .

 **...fairy cakes!**

"Delicious!" cried Monty.
"They're so fluttery,
and *FIZZY* and **SO** much
sweeter than people!
YUM!"

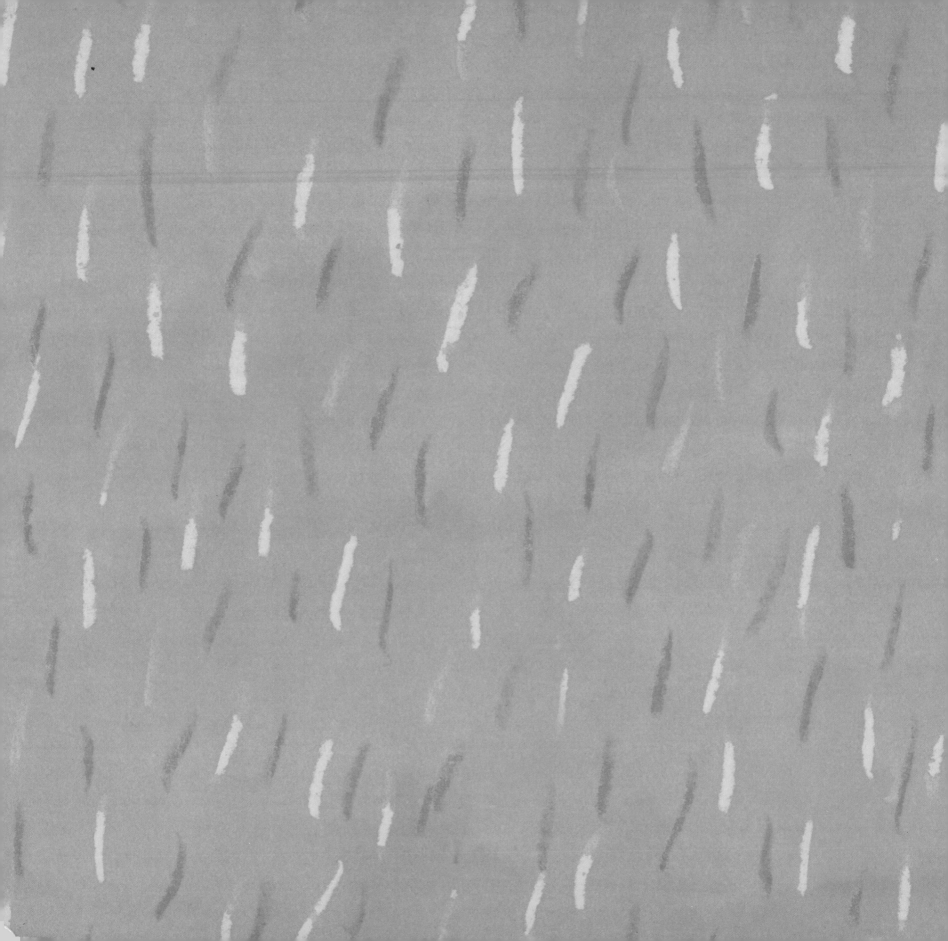